KT-512-168

FIFE LIBRARIES, CENTRAL AREA
WITHDRAWN

RADIO RESCUE

by
JOHN ESCOTT

Illustrated by Maureen Bradley

PUFFIN BOOKS

PUFFIN BOOKS

Published by the Penguin Group
27 Wrights Lane, London W8 5TZ, England
Viking Penguin Inc., 40 West 23rd Street, New York, New York 10010, USA
Penguin Books Australia Ltd, Ringwood, Victoria, Australia
Penguin Books Canada Ltd, 2801 John Street, Markham, Ontario, L3R 1B4
Penguin Books (NZ) Ltd, 182–190 Wairau Road, Auckland 10, New Zealand

Penguin Books Ltd, Registered Offices: Harmondsworth, Middlesex, England

First published by Hamish Hamilton Children's Books 1988
Published in Puffin Books 1990
1 3 5 7 9 10 8 6 4 2

Text copyright © John Escott, 1988
Illustrations copyright © Maureen Bradley, 1988
All rights reserved

Made and printed in Great Britain by
Richard Clay Ltd, Bungay, Suffolk
Filmset in Baskerville

Except in the United States of America,
this book is sold subject to the condition
that it shall not, by way of trade or otherwise,
be lent, re-sold, hired out, or otherwise circulated
without the publisher's prior consent in any form of
binding or cover other than that in which it is
published and without a similar condition
including this condition being imposed
on the subsequent purchaser

KIRKCALDY DISTRICT LIBRARIES

510656

JF

EX

Chapter 1

THE AUKSEA SIGN flashed by Mia as she sat in the front seat of the van, her feet curled under her.

Mia didn't read the sign. Mia didn't read anything she wasn't forced to read. She just knew the word on the sign had been Auksea because her father had said, "We're here." And there was the sea, grey and sullen through the rain which streamed down the windscreen.

Mia leaned forward and switched on the radio. She fiddled with the dial until she tuned into some music. Mia liked to have a radio playing whenever possible.

"Auksea's not a bad place when the sun's out," Mr Goodrich said. "The weather's bound to pick up sometime."

People had been saying this for ages, Mia thought. Now it was August and *still* the rain poured down. "If this keeps up, we'll need an ark not a caravan."

Her father laughed. "Two weeks," he said, reminding her how long they had together.

"Great," Mia said, grinning at him. She liked being with her father, she felt relaxed and comfortable.

Until a year ago, Mr Goodrich had been in the Navy and never home long enough for them to really enjoy one another's company or get to know each other properly. Now it was different. And in spite of the arguments he and Mia's mother had – often about Mia – Mia was glad he was home. Mrs Goodrich was her brother David's champion, Mia's father was hers.

"Don't forget we have to phone Mum," Mr Goodrich said. "She'll want to know we arrived safely."

Mia didn't want to think about home, not now, not when they were

3

seventy miles away. "She'll have taken David to his gymnastics class," Mia said. "He goes every Saturday."

Mr Goodrich smiled. "See? You *can* remember things."

Mia made a face, then laughed. He sometimes teased her about the way she forgot things. Forgot which day of the week it was, even which month of the year.

It made her mother furious. "You just don't *try*, Mia," Mrs Goodrich would say. "Think, girl. Use your brain." She said the word 'brain' as if she suspected Mia had been born without one.

There were times when Mia wondered about this herself.

The music on the radio ended and the voice of a woman presenter took its place.

"And that record was for Jamie Anderson of Myrtle Crescent. Happy birthday again, Jamie. Well, that's about all we have time for today. Now who's on Cruso's Island next week, Sam?"

"Next week's guest is Bobby Gruber, the comedian, Penny."

"Ah, yes. He's appearing at Auksea Pavilion the week after, isn't he?"

"That's right."

"Well, we have to be going now, but don't forget to send your competition entries to me,

Penny Cruso, Roundbay Radio, Auksea, by Thursday, please. And remember to join us again next week when my Crew – Donald, Tracy and Sam – will have lots of questions to ask Bobby Gruber, and there'll be record requests, book reviews, competitions and much more . . . "

The title music faded in.

" . . . so goodbye from me, Penny. And goodbye from Friday, our parrot . . . "

There was a loud squawk, followed by the flapping of wings.

" . . . and goodbye from the Crew."

"GOODBYE!"

Mia laughed. "Hey, I wish I could ask Bobby Gruber some questions, he's really funny. I watched his last TV series."

Mr Goodrich nodded. "Roundbay Radio, did she say? That must be the local radio station. First time I've heard

6

a programme where they have kids as presenters."

"Why shouldn't they?" Mia said. "I'd like to do it if . . . well, anyway I'd like to ask Bobby Gruber lots of things. Bet my questions would be better than that Sam and whoever else it was will ask."

Mr Goodrich began to look for a turning off the cliff road. "Keep your

eyes open for the Bay View Caravan Site," he said.

Mia began to feel excited in spite of the rain. They passed a house perched on the edge of the cliff, its windows boarded up and the remains of the garden – that which hadn't fallen over the cliff – clogged with thistles and spiky grass. It had a haunted look about it. Mia shivered with pleasure. She liked spooky things. At a funfair, it was always the ghost train she headed for.

"Over there," her father said, pointing to a side road and an arched entrance with caravans beyond.

Mia glanced at the sign over the entrance, picked out the word 'Bay' and ignored the rest.

"That's it!" she yelled, then let out an enormous WHOOP! of delight.

In the big general office at Roundbay Radio, Sam stood beside Penny Cruso's desk, a worried frown on his face. He was looking towards one of the smaller offices where he could see Penny talking to Mr Munford, the Programme Controller.

Or rather, Sam could see Penny *listening* to the tall, hatchet-faced man as Mr Munford spoke in jerky, irritated bursts, throwing occasional glances in Sam's direction.

Sam wondered what he had done wrong now.

Only the previous Saturday he had annoyed the Programme Controller by 'being rude' to the guest on *Cruso's Island*. At least, that's what Mr Munford said Sam had been. In fact, all Sam had done was ask the man – a vet, talking about the treatment of sick ani-

mals – why his charges were so high. It had seemed a perfectly reasonable question. Sam had gone to this particular vet with one of the visitors on his father's caravan site – Bay View Caravan Site – when the woman's dog had been injured by some broken glass on the beach. Sam had been shocked at the price the woman had been charged.

So, his question had seemed a fair one. But it turned out the vet was a personal friend of Mr Munford and because Sam's question had made the programme guest a bit uncomfortable, Mr Munford had called it 'rude'.

Penny had defended Sam. And she had defended Sam when Sam had told Mr Munford that, no, he didn't think his father would be interested in advertising Bay View Caravans on Roundbay Radio. After all, it was people in other parts of the country that Mr Peters wanted to reach with his advertising, not Auksea people.

But Mr Munford had been annoyed about that as well. So, one way and another, Sam wasn't very popular with the Programme Controller. Which was why he was worried when he saw Penny coming back with a rather solemn expression on her face.

Donald and Tracy had already left. Sam had waited behind to collect the books to be reviewed on next week's programme. He was doing the book reviews this month, something he enjoyed.

"What's the trouble?" Sam asked.

Penny hesitated, then said, "Mr Munford thinks we should have a fresh voice or two on the programme."

Sam's heart sank. This was it then,

the thing he had feared might happen. He was to be replaced on the programme. He had always known that if any of the Crew were to be replaced, it would probably be him. Tracy's father, Greg Wills, was another Roundbay Radio presenter, so it was unlikely that Tracy would be taken off. And Donald was the one with all the bright ideas for outside reporting and who to get as interesting guests on the programme.

Sam knew he was the least important of the three. "What did I do wrong today?" he asked.

Penny put an arm around Sam's shoulder. "Well, since you ask, you gave an unfavourable review of one of Mr Munford's favourite books."

Sam looked astonished. "Since when did Mr Munford read children's books?"

Penny smiled. "It was a favourite of his when he was a child. *Treasure Finders*, you remember you reviewed a new edition of it?"

"Oh, that one," Sam said. "I thought it was old-fashioned and boring."

"So you mentioned on the programme," Penny said.

"Well, you've always told us to say what we really think."

Penny nodded. "Quite right. It was just unfortunate you picked that book to be critical about. Anyway, Mr Munford has suggested we get a guest reviewer on next week's programme."

"Guest reviewer?"

"Some boy or girl," Penny said.

Who will eventually replace me, Sam thought, miserably. "Who will you get?" he asked.

"I was going to let you find somebody, Sam."

Find my own replacement; I see. Sam's spirits sank to an all-time low. "I can't think of anybody suitable right now," he said.

This wasn't true. Several of Sam's friends were keen readers but Sam didn't want them elbowing in on what he saw as his own special world of local radio.

Penny took two books from her drawer. "Just these, this week," she said.

Sam took the books. "I'd better go," he said. "There'll be some glum-looking holidaymakers turning up this morning. There always are when it's raining. As if they expect Dad to supply fine weather with each caravan."

Penny laughed. "If he could do that, Sam, he'd be a millionaire, and then you'd be so busy taking world cruises you wouldn't have time for *Cruso's Island*."

Sam took the remark seriously. "Yes, I would. I'd get Dad to buy up Roundbay Radio and then make *Cruso's Island* a daily programme instead of just once a week."

And Mr Misery Munford would be first to get the sack, he added silently in his head.

Chapter 2

OVER THE NEXT week, the weather hardly improved at all, but Mia and her father refused to be gloomy. They took long walks on the beach between the storms, wandered in and out of the tiny shops around the harbour and paid a visit to Auksea's one and only cinema.

"At this rate, we shan't have anything left to do next week," Mr Goodrich said.

"We can go and see Bobby Gruber at the Auksea Pavilion," Mia told him.

They phoned Mia's mother several times, using the phone in the camp site shop. On each occasion, Mia had a few words with her mother.

She sounds different, Mia thought. Not so prickly and snappy as she did when Mia was at home. But then, Mia thought, I'm not so prickly and snappy either.

"David has been entered in the Area Gymnastic Championships," Mrs Goodrich told Mia over the phone. "Isn't that wonderful?"

"Lovely," Mia said in a flat voice. She was pleased for David, of course. It was just that her mother never got excited about anything Mia did. Not that I ever do anything to get excited about, Mia thought gloomily.

"It's a good thing we didn't come with you and Daddy," Mrs Goodrich said. "If we'd been away, David wouldn't have had the chance to enter the trials and be selected, would he?"

"No," Mia said. But that's not the *only* reason you let Dad and me go off on our own, she thought. You and David just wanted a rest from having me around.

The Thursday after they arrived, Mia met Sam.

She had seen him serving behind the counter in the site shop, but had only said things like 'Hallo', and 'Lousy weather, isn't it?' to him. On Thursday evening, he came to their caravan.

Mia was watching TV, a small colour portable which came with the caravan her father had rented for the fortnight. Mr Goodrich was drinking a can of beer which he'd bought at the site shop that afternoon after their walk along the beach. A smear of foam marked his dark moustache each time he took the can away from his mouth.

He was writing a postcard to David. Slowly, painstakingly, the way he wrote everything. His handwriting was large and childlike.

Just then, there was a knock at the door of the caravan.

"Who's that?" Mia said, frowning.

"Open the door and we'll find out," Mr Goodrich said.

The boy from the site shop was standing in the rain. "I'm Sam," he said. "Sorry to bother you but my dad's car won't start and he wondered if your dad could spare a minute, just to take a quick look at it. Only we noticed the sign on your van. *Parker's Mobile Motor Repairs*."

Mia nodded. "My dad's a mechanic. His boss let us borrow the van for our holiday."

"Who are you keeping out in the rain, Mia?" Mr Goodrich called.

"Sorry," Mia said to Sam. "Come inside."

Mr Goodrich switched off the TV. "Hallo," he said to Sam. "You're Mr and Mrs Peters' son, aren't you?"

"That's right," Sam said, and explained about his father's car.

"'Course I'll take a look," Mr Goodrich said, swallowing the rest of his beer. "I expect it's just the damp affecting the leads or distributor."

Mia went with them. She was bored with the television.

The car was under a lean-to at the back of the shop. A frustrated Mr Peters stared at the engine under the open bonnet. Mr Goodrich smiled and went across.

Sam's mother popped her head out of

the back door of the shop and said, "Would you two like some ice-creams? They're not exactly selling well this weather."

So Mia followed Sam through to the front of the shop where Mrs Peters fished out two Choc-an'-Nut-Whoppers from the deep freeze.

"Want to play a game?" Sam asked Mia. "Your dad might be a little while."

"Uh – OK," Mia said, feeling a familiar twinge of anxiety.

"Come on then," Sam said. He led her up to his room over the shop.

It was small and cluttered. A cupboard door hung open and clothes and old toys spilled from it on to the carpet. On a table by the window, a half-finished model of the *Cutty Sark* was surrounded by tiny tins of paint and a squeezed-out tube of modelling cement. A heap of books stood beside the bed.

"'Scuse the mess," Sam said, reaching into the cupboard to unearth something.

Compared to her own room, Mia thought, this one was tidy.

You're so disorganised, Mia. It makes me want to scream with despair. Her mother's voice echoed in Mia's head. Mia *did* scream with despair when she was forced to tidy up, because the harder she tried to create some sort of order out of the chaos, the more bewildered she became.

Sam fished out a box. "Hope you like Scrabble," he said to Mia.

Mia's mouth went dry. She could hear her heartbeat suddenly, as though someone had turned up the volume.

Sam cleared a space on the floor and

26

unfolded the Scrabble board. Plastic letter-squares had come loose in the box and he gathered them up and put them in the canvas bag with all the others.

He held the bag out to Mia. "Pick a letter. Nearest to the beginning of the alphabet starts."

Mia licked her lips, clutching the half-melting Choc-an'-Nut-Whopper in one hand and trying to keep the other steady as she reached into the bag. She drew out a small square of plastic.

Sam did the same. "What've you got? Mine's an L."

Mia stared at the letter square and put it face up on the floor.

"S," Sam said. "So I start."

She had to do something. Anything. As long as it stopped them playing this loathsome game which would quickly reveal her secret.

27

Distract him, said the little voice inside Mia's head.

She had done it before, many times, whenever her weakness was in danger of being revealed to strangers. She would pretend to faint. Or cause some small accident. Or pretend to choke on something.

"Come on," Sam said. "Take your seven letters from the bag."

He held it out to her. Now, Mia thought.

And she dropped her Choc-an'-Nut-Whopper into the canvas bag.

"Hey!" Sam began.

"Sorry!" Mia cried. "Oh gosh, I'm so *sorry*." She stuffed a hand into the bag amongst the half-melted mess of chocolate and nuts – and *squeezed* the slimy remains. Ice-cream oozed between her fingers and spread itself all over the plastic letters. Then Mia removed her hand, letters stuck to both sides of it, and tried to scrub it clean with her handkerchief. "Oh, good heavens! I'm sorry . . . "

"Stop, for pete's sake," Sam said. "Come into the bathroom, you can wash it off." He screwed up his face. "Yeeuk!"

The canvas bag leaked chocolate ice-cream in a sticky trail along the hall carpet. Mia washed her hands, then Sam filled the basin with water and emptied the gooey squares into it.

"I think we'd better forget Scrabble." He stared at Mia as if he thought she might be crazy.

"Yes," Mia agreed. She made her face look suitably solemn.

They went back downstairs leaving the plastic letters floating in the water, now a creamy-brown colour. It was obvious Sam had been going to suggest some other game but had changed his mind. Mia didn't blame him. In fact, she was used to this happening.

She felt dismal. It would have been nice to have made a friend of Sam for the holiday but she had put paid to that, unless she could make amends in some way.

Mrs Peters looked surprised to see them back.

"Your father's got our car going," she told Mia, "but don't rush off. I think the two men are planning a celebratory drink at *The Anchor*, so why don't you stay?"

"No, it's all right," Mia said, noticing Sam's look of alarm. "I was – er – going to listen to a programme on the radio and I have to wash my hair."

She and Sam went outside.

"You want to listen to Roundbay Radio," he said. "It's the best station."

"It's the local station, isn't it?" Mia said.

Sam nodded. "Right."

It was then that Mia remembered the programme she'd heard that first morning when they had been driving along the cliff top. "Hey, there was a boy called Sam talking about Bobby Gruber last Saturday, on this kids' programme, and – "

"That was me," Sam said.

"Really?" And here, Mia realised, was her chance to make it up to Sam for ruining his Scrabble set.

"Hey, isn't that *amazing*?" she said, popping open her eyes. "Gosh, I've always wanted to be on a radio programme. What's it like? Do you have to

32

wear headphones? Do they have red lights that flash when you're on the air?"

Sam tried to look modest – and failed. "It's nothing special," he lied.

"Oh, but it must be *fantastic*." Mia knew she was overdoing it but she had to lead Sam's thoughts away from her own 'peculiar' behaviour, as Sam would see it. She had to wipe out the memory of the chocolate-stained letters somehow and this, as she had learned from experience, was one way of doing it. "I'd give anything to be on, especially with Bobby Gruber. I think you're ever so lucky, Sam. How did it start?"

"Penny Cruso rented a caravan here when she first came," Sam explained, pleased to have a new audience for the story he never tired of repeating. "She has a flat now, but at first she had nowhere to stay and came here."

"Gosh," Mia said, relieved that her dodge seemed to be working.

"Yes, well anyway, she mentioned she was going to be a presenter on Roundbay Radio, the new local station, and that she would be starting this children's programme and would be needing a team of two or three presenters."

"And she asked you?"

"I was the first of the Crew to be recruited," Sam said proudly.

"Wow," Mia said, wondering how she could politely get away before he suggested going to see if the Scrabble letters were dry. "Anyway, I'd give anything to go on a programme like that. Gosh, yes. But look, I have to go now so I'll see you around sometime. OK?"

"Oh – ?"

"'Bye then." Mia walked off quickly before he had a chance to say any more. After a few steps, she broke into a jog.

It was only when she got inside the caravan that Mia realised she was shaking all over.

Moments later, she was sick.

Sam went back to his room after Mia had gone.

What an odd girl, he thought. Why all that nonsense with the Scrabble? Sam had no doubts that Mia had done it on purpose. Crazy, he decided. A nutter. Look at the way she went on about *Cruso's Island*. Really over the top, that had been.

And then he had an idea. That was it! He would ask *her* to do the book reviews. Hadn't she said she would give anything to be on a radio programme like *Cruso's Island*?

So he would do her a favour, wouldn't he? She could be the guest reviewer. Sam smiled. Because there was no danger of Mia becoming a permanent fixture on the programme; she was only here for two weeks.

Yes, she would do nicely.

Chapter 3

MIA'S FATHER HAD decided to lie on in bed. He had peeked out of the caravan window, seen there was no sun, and turned over to go back to sleep.

Mia didn't mind. Her father got up early when he was working so why shouldn't he lie in when he was on holiday?

Although there was no sun, it was a dry morning with ivory-coloured clouds scudding across the sky. Mia pulled on a sweater and some jeans and went for a walk.

She took the path which led to the

cliff road and on down to the beach. It was steep and twisting and went past a field where some new houses were being built.

Auksea was a place of the very old and the very new, Mia thought. As if nothing had been done for years and then, suddenly, someone had given the order for new developments to take place and the whole town had woken up.

One of the 'old' bits came into view after Mia had walked half a mile along the nearly empty beach. It was the house with the boarded windows which she had noticed that first morning when they had been driving along the cliff road. From the beach, it looked more sad than haunted.

There were wooden steps coming from the crumbling garden but they

finished half-way down the cliff where the ground beneath them had collapsed.

And yet, Mia saw, there was another route up to what remained of the steps. Going from another angle, across the sandstone rocks, you could reach them and then climb on to the house itself. Something which you couldn't get to from the cliff road because the property was boarded off with a high fence.

Mia had half decided to try and make the climb when the first spots of rain began to fall.

She groaned. "Not *more* rain."

She turned and followed her own footprints back along the wet sand. Then she took two wrong turnings and ended up going round in a circle before calming herself down and starting again. Mia often lost her way and, over the years, had learned not to panic. It was knowing her left from her right that was the problem, something Mia had never been able to master.

By the time Mia finally reached the caravan site, her sweater and jeans were soaked.

"Hey, Mia!" somebody shouted.

She turned and saw Sam waving from the shop doorway. Please, she prayed silently, don't let him ask me to play Scrabble again.

"I went for a walk and it started to rain," she said, stepping into the shop.

He looked at her wet clothes.

"So I have to go and change," she added, just in case he got any ideas about board games.

"Remember you said you'd like to be on *Cruso's Island*?" Sam said.

"Oh yes," Mia said, relieved that

41

was all he wanted to talk about. "It sounds a smashing programme. You're very lucky to be a part of it, Sam." She smiled at him and nodded encouragingly.

Part of Mia's problem was that people thought her different. Odd, or even stupid. And, naturally, this put them off her. Mia knew this and had learned that it helped if you were well-liked and popular, and she made determined and sometimes extreme efforts to get on with others.

"Yes, well," Sam went on, "you can be part of the programme, too."

"I can?"

"Just for this Saturday," Sam said.

"Great!" Mia said. "Bobby Gruber is on. I can ask him lots of questions."

Sam then produced the two books which he had been holding behind his back. The top one had a castle on the front cover. "You'll also have to read these and do reviews on the programme," he said. "You're going to be a guest reviewer, see."

The grin on Mia's face became fixed. She stared at the objects in Sam's hand as if they were tarantula spiders.

"I know it doesn't give you long, but — what's the matter?" Sam asked. "You're shaking. Are you cold?"

Mia nodded, still staring at the books.

"You should get out of those wet clothes." Sam pushed the books into her hand. "Take these with you and read them. They're only short and it won't take you long. The programme starts at eight o'clock, so meet me outside the shop at half-past seven, OK?"

Mia nodded again, still unable to speak.

Sam laughed. "Don't look so worried, they're only books. You can read, can't you?"

Mia forced a little laugh. "'Course I can."

Sam went back into the shop and she walked back to the caravan. A weight seemed to have settled in the pit of her stomach.

Her mother had shelves full of books, all over the house. David, her brother, had loads too. They towered over Mia like hundreds of bogeymen, waiting to trap her, waiting to make her look foolish.

Whenever she was faced with printed words – in books, newspapers, magazines, on signs or labels – Mia's brain seemed to unravel like a ball of string until the inside of her head was a tangle of loops and painful knots. Even her stomach ached sometimes.

"It's just *laziness*, Mia," her mother said in an exasperated voice whenever Mia tried to explain this. "You just don't try hard enough."

It was hard explaining anything to her mother if it took more than a few minutes. Mrs Goodrich's life was filled with activities – clubs, committees, and her job as a supervisor at a large department store. And then there was David. He had to be ferried around to his gymnastics competitions and coaching, his clarinet lessons and scout meetings. There wasn't a lot of time left for coping with 'difficult' daughters.

Mia glanced at the books Sam had given her. There were a lot of pictures in them. Maybe if she looked long enough it would be possible to work out what they were about. Enough to say something about them. Pretend she'd read them, in other words.

But Mia knew she couldn't. Not on the radio. Not even for the chance to talk with Bobby Gruber, her favourite funny-man.

Not for *anything*.

Chapter 4

MIA OFTEN FORGOT appointments. She
would arrange to meet somebody at a
certain time, a certain place – and then
forget all about it. Her friends were
used to this. And because Mia was good
at thinking up new things to do, they
forgave her.

Mia wished she could have forgotten
about her meeting with Sam on
Saturday morning. It was cruel the way
you forgot the things you wanted to
remember, but the things you wanted
to forget you just couldn't.

Seven-thirty, he'd told her. Outside the shop.

At seven-fifteen on the Saturday morning of the programme, Mia sneaked out of the caravan park and headed for the beach. She took her radio for company and, inside her anorak pocket, the two books. Just in

case . . . what? That she changed her mind? Mia didn't think so.

Her father had been sleeping when she left the caravan. She had left him a note. 'Gone for a walk.' At least, Mia thought that was what she had written, she could never be sure.

She walked along the beach, her radio playing, a lone figure in the rain.

She felt sick. Sick at how she'd let Sam down, sick because she couldn't do a simple little thing like read a book, then say a few words about it.

At school she was given only the simplest books to read. Babyish, they were, and Mia became bored with them quickly. "I'm beginning to think you need some extra help which I can't give you, Mia," her teacher had said last term. "I must have a word with your mother." But, so far, Mia's mother hadn't seen the teacher.

The trouble was, Mia *felt* stupid. At times, she wanted to run away and hide from everybody. Like now. Like this very moment when she felt so badly about letting Sam down. She would have to stay away from the caravan site until the programme was over.

But she would have to face Sam sometime. And tell him what? Well, that was easy. She forgot. Good old Mia always forgets things. Ask anybody.

She was getting wetter by the moment. Where could she shelter?

As if in answer, Mia caught sight of the house on the cliff, visible through the misty rain. Its boarded windows and sagging roof gave it a cheerless, wretched look.

"Just the way I feel," Mia said to herself.

At least she would be alone there as well as dry, she decided, heading towards the sandstone rocks and the rickety wooden steps.

She was halfway up the cliffside when one of the two books fell out of her pocket and slithered back down behind her. Mia watched it for a moment, then climbed on without giving it another thought.

She passed a sign but ignored it, the way she ignored all signs.

If she had been able to read it, Mia would have learned that it said: SUB-SIDENCE! CLIFF DANGEROUS! KEEP AWAY!

But Mia didn't read signs.

Sam couldn't understand what had happened. He had told the girl he would meet her at seven-thirty but at seven-fifteen, whilst Sam was gulping down a bowl of cornflakes, he had seen Mia going out of the site entrance, clutching her radio.

He straight away assumed she had misunderstood and had gone to the Studios direct, not waiting for him. But when Sam arrived at Roundbay Radio, there was no sign of Mia.

"Hallo, Sam," Penny said.

"Hi, Sam," Donald and Tracy said.

"Hallo," Sam said. He looked across the general office to see Mr Munford crossing the room towards them.

"Where's your guest reviewer, Sam?" Penny asked.

"I – I haven't got one," Sam admitted.

"What's this?" Mr Munford said, joining them. "No guest reviewer?"

"Oh dear," Penny said. "And Bobby

53

Gruber has just phoned to say he won't be able to get here either. He's stuck in a traffic jam the other side of Exeter."

Mr Munford looked as if he'd like to step on somebody. "So we are going to have a right mess-up of a programme this morning, are we?"

"I've got a report I can do on the Marinelife Aquarium," Donald said. "I was saving it until next week but I can do it today."

"And we can always fill up with record requests," Tracy said.

"I'm sure Sam will do the book reviews as usual this week, Mr Munford," Penny said. "Then he can find a reviewer for next Saturday."

"But I can't," Sam said miserably.

"Pardon?" Penny said.

"I can't do the reviews," Sam said. "I don't have the books."

"I think you'd better explain, Sam," Penny said.

Sam did. "Why do people do things like that?" he said when he had finished. "Why say you want to come on a programme if you don't really want to? And what about the books I gave her to review? The least she could have done was given them back."

"The fact is," Mr Munford told Sam, "you have let us down badly." He turned to Penny. "Now perhaps you see what I mean about having somebody new on the programme. Come and see me afterwards and we'll discuss it."

He turned and marched back to his office. Donald, Tracy and Penny watched him.

Sam couldn't see anything. His eyes were blurred with tears. After a moment, he turned and ran out of the

office, down the stairs and out of the
Studios altogether.

"Sam!" Penny shouted after him.

Sam didn't even turn round.

Chapter 5

MIA GOT INTO the house through a window. The nails in the boards covering the window had come out of the rotting frame, and Mia was easily able to prise them away.

The rain beat against her back as she climbed through. Water streamed down the path at the side of the building, gathered into whirlpools when it reached the cracks in the garden, then rushed on over the edge of the cliff in small waterfalls.

Chunks of the ground went with it. Unnoticed by Mia, several tumbled

away at the opposite corner of the building, like lumps of icing falling from around the base of a cake.

Mia screwed up her nose. "Pooh! It smells damp and mildewy."

The only daylight came from the window behind her. Plaster had dropped from the walls and a fireplace at the other end leaned off-centre. There was a huge crack behind it, going up the wall and across the ceiling to a point above Mia's head. It looked big enough to put your arm in.

Most of the floorboards had gone and Mia moved carefully towards the doorway which led into the hall beyond. The stairs, which had curved down from the floor above, now hung like loose teeth, dangling precariously over the black hole which had once been the floor.

It was only then it occurred to Mia that she might have wandered into somewhere that wasn't safe.

She retreated back into the first room, her radio playing and echoing around her. It was company. The only other sound was that of the rain beating against the boarded windows like some angry monster trying to break in.

"And you can stop thinking thoughts like that," Mia told herself sharply. "It's only a house, for heaven's sake. Somebody lived here once."

She sat on the floor and listened as the opening music of *Cruso's Island* filled the room. Mia wasn't at all sure she wanted to hear this, reminding her of what she'd done. She was about to twiddle the knob to find another station . . . and then it happened. An enormous creaking, *groaning* sound from another part of the building, and Mia felt the floor beneath her move.

She screamed.

But the scream was sucked into the thunderous roar of the whole house splitting in two. Mia looked up and saw the crack in the ceiling above her widen. The plaster began to fall in great slabs.

And then everything went black.

Sam couldn't go home. His parents would be listening to *Cruso's Island*, the way they always did, and wondering why he wasn't on it.

It was that girl's fault!

Sam wanted to go to the Goodrich caravan and see if she had come back so that he could ask her what she'd been playing at, getting him into trouble and losing him his place on the Crew.

But it would have to wait. He couldn't bear to see his parents or anybody else just yet, nor get within listening distance of any radio until the programme was over.

It would be the first time since *Cruso's Island* began that Sam hadn't been part of it, and he felt sick. He wanted to crawl into a deep hole and hide.

Instead, he walked along the beach in the pouring rain. There was only one other person about, a woman with an Alsatian dog. She wore black wellingtons and a long hooded coat, her hands thrust deep into the pockets. The dog romped happily along the edge of the sea.

The woman looked surprised to see Sam.

"I *had* to come out in the rain," she said as she caught him up. "If Kit doesn't get his morning run, I get no peace for the rest of the day. But what on earth are you doing walking in this weather?"

She had a nice smile and Sam almost told her, then changed his mind. "I – just felt like it," he said.

The woman had been about to say something else when they both heard the noise. A rumbling, creaking, crashing noise at the other end of the empty beach. Kit heard it too, and began running in that direction.

"The old house!" the woman cried. "Look! The ground's going from under it!"

They both watched, fascinated, as half the building collapsed and tumbled in a tide of bricks and sand, following the garden which had already crashed its way down to the beach.

The landslide lasted less than a minute, then a huge cloud of dust rose up from the heap of rubble at the foot of the cliff. The half-building above looked ready to follow any second.

"Kit, come back!" the woman shouted.

Sam watched the dog race towards the pile of broken bricks and masonry as the woman hurried after it. Sam jogged after her.

"Thank heavens there was nobody on the beach at this point," the woman

said when they reached the mound of
rubble.

66

"Lucky the rain kept people away," Sam agreed.

"Except it was probably the heavy rain which finally did the damage," the woman said. "The ground has been sinking under that old place for ages, that's why the warning signs were put there. All this rain over the past few weeks must have been the final straw."

The dog began to scramble up the cliff towards the wooden steps which now led nowhere.

"Kit!" called the woman. "Come

here. What are you sniffing at?"

Sam looked round as the dog moved something with its nose. The object slithered down the cliffside and Kit chased it.

It was a book. A new book, soaked by the rain. It had a castle on the front cover.

Sam gave a small gasp as he recognised it. He looked up at the broken steps, then down at the remains of the house on the beach.

"What is it?" the woman said. "You've gone as white as a sheet."

"I – I think somebody might have been in the house," he said.

"*What*?" Alarm spread across the woman's face. "But – Kit!" She gave an exasperated shout after the dog which had now headed back up the cliffside. "What is he after now?"

Suddenly, the dog began to howl. An odd, wailing noise.

"Why's he doing that?" Sam asked.

The woman frowned. "It's the noise he makes when he hears the TV or radio at home. How odd." She looked up at the half of the old house still standing. "Do – do you think there could be a radio playing up there?"

"Radio?" echoed Sam.

And then he remembered what Mia had been clutching as she had left the site that morning.

Chapter 6

MIA OPENED HER eyes, felt the rain on her face and heard music blaring.

She looked up and saw a patch of dark cloud move slowly across the hole in the roof. The ceiling of the room Mia was in lay around her on the floor. The piece of plasterboard which had briefly knocked her out sat in her lap. Plaster dust had settled in a thin film over her whole body and Mia could taste it on her lips.

She tried to get up and a sharp pain shot through her head. Mia winced and closed her eyes. When she opened them

again, the pain had subsided to a dull ache above her left eye.

She knew what had happened. At least, she thought she did. The house where she had gone to hide – but *why* had she been hiding? – had collapsed. The ceiling had fallen in on her.

Then she recalled where the house was, on the cliffside, and remembered why she had come there. Remembered *Cruso's Island* and Sam.

And the books.

She had to get out, her father would be worried. Besides, Mia now knew she had been wrong to come to this place. She scrambled across heaps of brick and plaster and wood, feet slipping and sliding into cracks and openings. Her whole head throbbed and tiny stars of light appeared on the fringes of her vision.

There was no way back through the window she had entered. A door from an upstairs room was wedged tightly across the front of it, hemmed in by a heap of bricks. She would have to go the other way, into the hall.

Mia climbed over lumps of brick and timber until she reached the doorway – *and stared into space*. There was nowhere to go. Just a sheer drop down the cliff to the beach.

Mia screamed for the second time that morning.

Down below, somebody shouted, "Up there!"

The woman gasped, her hands going to her face.

"Mia!" Sam shouted. But his voice was carried away by the wind. The girl, white-faced and tiny in the distance, moved back into the building.

"She can't hear you," the woman said to Sam. "Quickly, we must get help. The rest of the house could come down any moment."

"She'll be terrified," Sam said. "If only I could talk to her."

"I'll get the police, the ambulance, *somebody*," said the woman. "You – "

"I'll stay here in case she comes out again," Sam said. "Perhaps I can make her hear next time, tell her somebody's coming to rescue her."

"She'll never hear you in all this wind," the woman said. "It took Kit's highly sensitive ears to pick up a snatch of her radio, remember."

Radio.

"I know how I can talk to her!" Sam shouted, and he began running back along the beach.

Chapter 7

"HALLO AGAIN. *This is Cruso's Island, back after the break. Now before we go on, I must tell you Sam's arrived and he seems to have some important news. Sam?"*

"I've just come from the beach, Penny. The old guest house on the east cliff has collapsed and half of it has fallen over the side."

"Good gracious, Sam! I hope nobody was underneath."

"I don't think so, but there's somebody in the remaining half of the house — and she's trapped."

"But — Sam, I — we must alert the rescue services — "

"Somebody's already doing that, they'll be on the way by now. But it will be a little while before anybody actually gets to Mia — that's the name of the girl who's trapped — and I thought we could talk to her while she's waiting. I thought it might make her feel less lonely up there."

"Talk to her? But how?"

"She's got her radio with her – that's how we first knew she was there – and I think she's listening to Cruso's Island. Is that right, Mia . . . ?"

Mia stared at the transistor, laying amongst lumps of plaster, out of her reach. Something must have knocked against the volume control knob because it was playing at full volume, almost deafening in the wrecked room.

Mia listened to Sam's voice as if it was magic. She almost wanted to laugh. Instead, she began to cry, but they were tears of relief.

Somebody knew she was up here. Somebody was coming to rescue her, wasn't that what he was saying? She only half-listened to Sam's words, just being able to hear his voice was enough, made her feel less alone.

" . . . *no need to be frightened, Mia. You'll be back at the caravan site in no time. So just hang on there. And Mia, don't move around. They say it's safer if you don't move around. Somebody will come and get you . . .* "

On and on went Sam's voice, soothing and relaxing. Mia began to feel calmer. Somebody was coming. It was going to be all right. Sam had said so.

And then she heard a helicopter.

On the beach below, a crowd had formed. Some clutched radios, pressing them against their ears as they listened

to Sam's voice. Above, a helicopter hovered like a dragonfly as one of the air-sea rescue team was lowered in a harness towards the house.

It took another agonising ten minutes to get Mia out. Strapped tightly in the harness, she was gathered up into the safety of the helicopter.

Unaware of all this, Sam talked on, his voice drifting up from the radios on the beach.

" . . . *don't worry, Mia. Everything is going to be all right* . . . "

Chapter 8

SAM AND PENNY sat in the waiting room at Auksea General Hospital's Accident Department. With them sat Mr Goodrich, pale with shock, holding a cup of tea which a nurse had given him.

He had known nothing about what had happened on the beach until a policeman turned up at the caravan. He had slept late, then got up to see Mia's note about going for a walk. He had assumed she would be back any moment, was even frying eggs and bacon when the policeman arrived.

By that time, Mia was safely at the

hospital and the policeman brought Mr Goodrich directly there.

Neither had he heard Sam's broadcast, although judging by the number of phone calls Roundbay Radio had received after it, Mr Goodrich was one of the few people in Auksea who *hadn't* heard it. Many had called in to praise Sam for his soothing but cheerful messages to Mia over the radio. In fact, Sam was something of a hero, although he couldn't understand why.

Now, as Mr Goodrich sipped his tea, he said, "Mia never reads signs, you see."

Penny and Sam looked at him in surprise.

"How do you mean, Mr Goodrich?" Penny said.

"She wouldn't have read the warning signs telling her to keep away from that

82

place," Mr Goodrich explained, "because she doesn't read signs."

"But why?" Sam asked.

"She has trouble with her reading," Mr Goodrich said. He looked at Sam suddenly, then asked, "What exactly was Mia supposed to do on that programme of yours? You say you asked her on but that she ran off at the last moment."

"She was going to review . . . some books . . . Oh."

Mr Goodrich nodded. "I see. Well, you weren't to know."

"Know what, Mr Goodrich?" Penny asked.

Mr Goodrich sighed. "That Mia is . . . well anyway, I *think* she is . . . dyslexic."

"Diswhat?" Sam said.

Penny gave Mr Goodrich an understanding look. "Dyslexic, Sam. It means Mia suffers from dyslexia. It's what is sometimes called word blindness and means Mia has lots of extra problems with reading and writing, amongst other things. It's more common than you think. I have a cousin – he's grown up now – and he's dyslexic. You can get help you know," she added to Mr Goodrich.

"I do know," he said. "It's something I've meant to – well – the thing is, Mia's mother won't accept there is anything wrong. She thinks Mia's lazy about reading, but there are other things, as I've tried to point out. The way Mia tends to lose her way, can't tell left from right. How she forgets things. Dyslexics have these sort of difficulties."

"I know," Penny said. "I can

remember Tom, my cousin, having similar problems. But he's much better now."

"I was the same when I was a kid," Mr Goodrich said. "Only nobody called it dyslexia then, they just thought I was a bit slow, a bit thick. But I wasn't, and neither is Mia. She's a bright kid, Miss Cruso."

"I'm sure she is," Penny said. "I remember reading that dyslexics, apart from their own special problems, are often more intelligent than other children."

Mr Goodrich put his cup and saucer on the floor in front of him, then straightened up. "It's been difficult for Mia's mum, you know, bringing up two children with me away in the Navy. Never home long enough to sort things out, realise what the problem was with

Mia." He looked embarrassed suddenly. "And me and my wife – well, we've had our difficulties, getting used to my being home all the time now. You know what it's like. It's hard just talking to each other sometimes, never mind sorting out Mia's problem. But she'll get help from now on, I promise you. Her mother will see how important it is when she hears about this." He shuddered. "When I think how close Mia came to . . . "

Penny put a hand on Mr Goodrich's arm. "Mia's safe now, and that's what is important."

At that moment, the nurse came out

of one of the curtained-off bays at the end of the room. She walked over to Mr Goodrich.

"Everything's all right," she said. "No bones broken, just a slight concussion. Mia will be fine tomorrow. You can go and see her if you like."

Mr Goodrich got up and hurried towards the other side of the room.

Sam gave a low whistle. "Fancy not reading warning signs. Wow, that really is dangerous."

"Mia would have avoided reading *anything*, Sam," Penny said. "But even if she'd tried to read the signs, she would probably have *misread* them. And Mia would have been upset, remember. She had let you down and didn't know how she was going to explain herself."

"Think we'll be able to explain it to Mr Munford?" Sam asked. "Think he'll let me stay on the programme?"

Penny smiled and put an arm around Sam's shoulder. "Stop worrying about Mr Munford. You're *Cruso's Island*'s young hero and Mr Munford knows it. He'll be telling everybody what a wonderful little broadcaster you are by now."

Sam grinned. "Could Mia come on next week's programme? Not as a reviewer, of course."

"Of course she can," Penny said. "Bobby Gruber will be on and she can interview him."

"That'll please her," Sam said.

"Then she can tell us about her rescue," Penny said. "And her radio rescuer!" And she plonked a kiss on Sam's head.

Sam's face turned as red as a traffic light.

RADIO ALERT
RADIO DETECTIVE
RADIO REPORTERS
John Escott

Three more exciting stories also centred round the local radio station, Roundbay Radio. There's a mystery in each story which the children involved help to solve brilliantly.

RAGDOLLY ANNA'S CIRCUS
Jean Kenward

Made only from a morsel of this and a tatter of that, Ragdolly Anna is a very special doll and the six stories in this book are all about her adventures.

SEE YOU AT THE MATCH
Margaret Joy

Six delightful stories about football. Whether spectator, player, winner or loser these short, easy stories for young readers are a must for all football fans.

THE GHOST AT NO. 13
Gyles Brandreth

Hamlet Brown's sister, Susan, is just too perfect. Everything she does is praised and Hamlet is in despair – until a ghost comes to stay for a holiday and helps him to find an exciting idea for his school project!

ONE NIL
Tony Bradman

Dave Brown is mad about football and when he learns that the England squad are to train at the local City ground he thinks up a brilliant plan to overcome his parent's objections and get him to the ground to see them.

ON THE NIGHT WATCH
Hannah Cole

A group of children and their parents occupy their tiny school in an effort to prevent its closure.

FIONA FINDS HER TONGUE
Diana Hendry

At home Fiona is a chatterbox but whenever she goes out she just won't say a word. How she overcomes her shyness and 'finds her tongue' is told in this charming book.

IT'S TOO FRIGHTENING FOR ME!
Shirley Hughes

The eerie old house gives Jim and Arthur the creeps. But somehow they just can't resist poking around it, even when a mysterious white face appears at the window! A deliciously scary story – for brave readers only!

THE CONKER AS HARD AS A DIAMOND
Chris Powling

Last conker season Little Alpesh had lost every single game! But this year it's going to be different and he's going to be Conker Champion of the Universe! The trouble is, only a conker as hard as a diamond will make it possible – and where on earth is he going to find one?